The Three Little Pigs

ILLUSTRATED BY
NINA BARBARESI

GOLDEN PRESS • NEW YORK
Western Publishing Company, Inc., Racine, Wisconsin

Once upon a time there were three little pigs who lived in a house in the woods with their mother.

One day the mother pig said to her children, "You are old enough to go out into the world and seek your fortunes."

The three little pigs packed their bags and said good-bye
to their mother. Then each little pig took a different path
and went out into the wide world.

The first little pig had not gone far when he met a man with a load of straw. "Please, sir," he said, "will you give me some straw to build a house?"

The man gave the little pig some straw.

Quick as a wink, the first little pig
built himself a straw house.

He did not know that a wicked wolf was
watching him from behind a tree.

The first little pig was barely settled in his new house
when the wolf came knocking at the door.

"Little pig, little pig, let me in, let me in,"
he called.

"Not by the hair of my chinny, chin, chin," answered the little pig. "I will not let you in."

"If you don't," said the wolf, "I'll huff and I'll puff and I'll blow your house down."

But the little pig would not open the door.

So the wolf huffed and he puffed and he blew the house down—and ate up the first little pig.

The second little pig had not gone far
when he met a man with a load of sticks.
"Please, sir," he said, "will you give me
some sticks to build a house?"

The man gave the little pig some sticks.

Quick as two winks, the second little pig
built himself a stick house.

He did not know that the wicked wolf was watching
him from behind a bush.

The second little pig was barely settled in his new house when the wolf came knocking at the door.

"Little pig, little pig, let me in, let me in," he called.

"Not by the hair of my chinny, chin, chin," answered the little pig.

"If you don't," said the wolf, "I'll huff and I'll puff and I'll blow your house down."

But the little pig
would not open
the door.

So the wolf huffed and he puffed, and he puffed
and he huffed, and he blew the house down—
and ate up the second little pig.

The third little pig had not gone
far when he met a man with a load of
bricks. "Please, sir," he said, "will you
give me some bricks to build a
house?"

The man gave the little pig
some bricks.

Slowly but surely, the third
little pig built himself
a brick house.

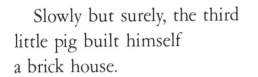

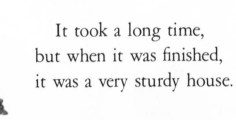

It took a long time,
but when it was finished,
it was a very sturdy house.

The little pig did not know
that the wicked wolf was watching him
from behind a big rock.

The third little pig was barely settled in his new house when the wolf came knocking at the door.

"Little pig, little pig, let me in, let me in," he called.

"Not by the hair of my chinny, chin, chin," answered the little pig.

"Then I'll huff and I'll puff and I'll blow your house down," said the wolf.

So the wolf huffed . . .

and he puffed . . .

and he huffed . . .

and he puffed . . .

. . . and he huffed and puffed some more. But try as he might, he could not blow that brick house down.

Then the wolf climbed up to the roof
and called down the chimney,
"Little pig, little pig, I am coming
down the chimney to eat you up!"

"That's what you think!" said the little pig.

The wolf came down the chimney and—SPLASH—he
fell right into the pot of water boiling over the fire.

The little pig popped the lid on the pot—and that was
the end of the wicked wolf!